The Tortoise and the Hare

and the Hare

Continued...

For Holly, Gracie and Finn

Discover Writing Press
PO Box 264
Shoreham, VT 05770
1-800-613-8055
Fax # 802-897-2084
www.discoverwriting.com
TEACHERS: For lesson ideas using this book visit our web site.

ISBN # 1-931492-01-8
O8 07 06 05 04 03 02   10 9 8 7 6 5 4 3 2 1

The Tortoise and the Hare Continued...

Original story by Aesop 600 BC revised by Barry Lane 2002 AD

Illustrated by Miles Bodimeade

DISCOVER WRITING PRESS

www.discoverwriting.com

You probably already think you know the story of the Tortoise and Hare. You know, how the slow and steady tortoise challenges the speedy hare to a race and then ends up winning because the hare goofs off and falls asleep when he should be racing. You probably think you know the moral too: Slow and steady wins the race.

Maybe your mother told you this story one night when you rushed through your homework or stuffed all the junk from the floor of your room into the closet instead of taking the time to clean it properly. Grown ups do enjoy stories which tell children how to behave, but they sometimes leave out the stuff which might confuse you.

Take the tortoise and the hare, for example. Did you ever hear what happened the next day?

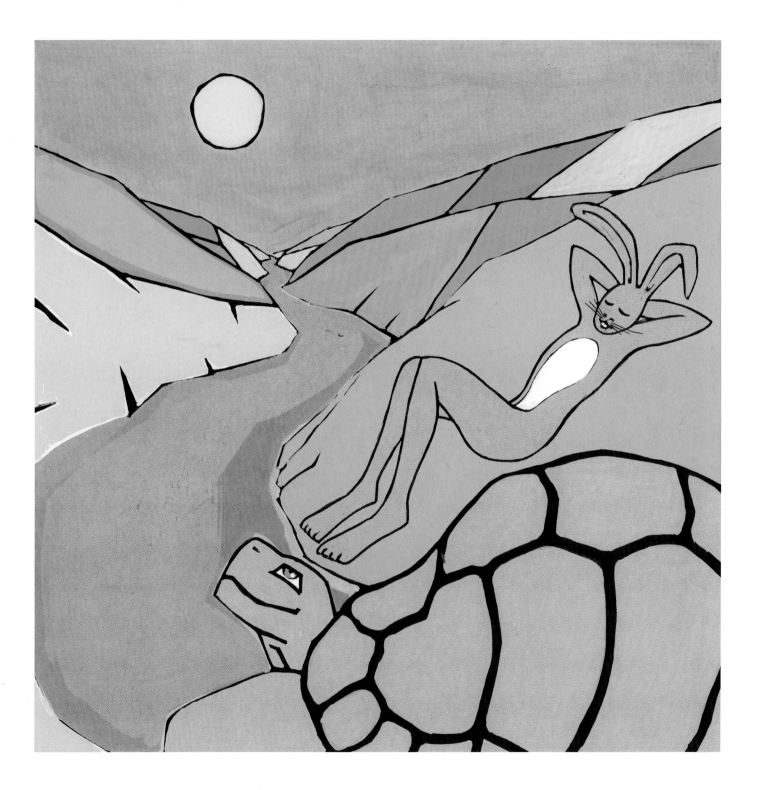

Well, the tortoise was really proud of himself. He thought he was something special. After all, he had changed the way people saw tortoises for all time. He was hot stuff. He appeared on the TV news and told of his victory. He described in great detail how he outwitted the slow-thinking hare. He was given medals and even hired by a company to sell their running shoes.

Then, of course, it happened.

It had to happen.

A group of five hares met the tortoise one day when he was relaxing on the beach.

"Hey speedy," the first hare quipped. "We hear you never really won that race. Heard you slipped our friend some kind of sleeping potion."

"Nonsense," laughed the tortoise. "Don't you hare brains ever learn? I won that race fair and square."

"I don't think so," said the hare. "If you're so sure, why don't you have another race and we'll see who's fastest now, Shellbreath."

"Well, maybe I'll just have to do that," replied the tortoise.

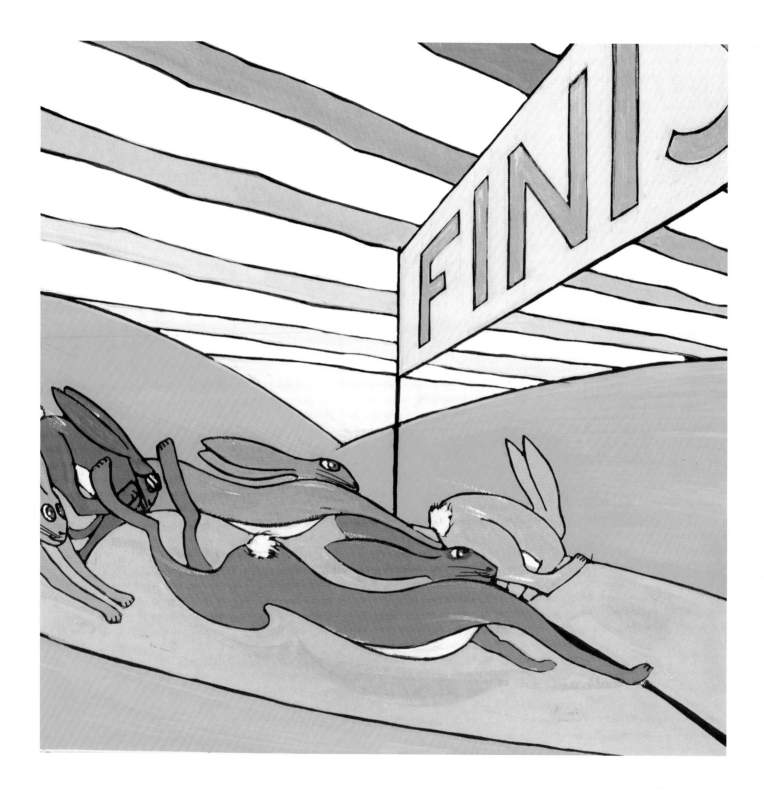

You can probably guess what happened next. Yes, the tortoise raced all five hares, but this time the hares were ready, and they crossed the finish line before the tortoise could make ten steps.

Moral: Quit while you're ahead.

How nice it would be if stories would just end, and we wouldn't have to think about them any more. But that's not the way life works. You see, there's always a next day, a next year, a next decade, and if you are a real reader, you know how to read past the words on the page to the new stories that blossom between the lines.

Oh these hares, they were so proud of themselves and started telling everyone how they had outwitted the slow–thinking tortoise. They went on TV talk shows, and won awards for America's most quick-thinking rodents. They were on the front cover of *Bunny Times.* Word got back to the tortoises, who decided to get revenge.

Ten tortoises, at a secret meeting, came up with a plan. They sent a formal letter to the hares challenging them to another race. The hares accepted and didn't seem to notice that some of these ten tortoises had furry legs. You see, the tortoises' secret plan was to hire a group of speedy gophers and dress them up as tortoises. The fake tortoises inched along till they got near the finish line; then they startled the hares and sprinted by them.

Moral: Cheating can sometimes work.

Wait a minute. That's not a moral. Can you think of a better one?

What about:

Never judge a tortoise by its shell alone.

You don't think the story ends here, do you?

When the hares found out that the tortoises had cheated they got mad. A call went out to all able–bodied hares to race the tortoises again. But this time the gophers knew they couldn't help, because a new rule was made which required all tortoise shells to be inspected before the race.

It looked bad for the tortoises. How could they ever win a race against a whole army of speedy hares? That's when the unexpected happened; halfway through the race a giant hailstorm broke out. Hailstones the size of grapefruits rained from the sky. The hares all ran for cover, in caves, under rocks, and into burrows. The tortoises, with their suits of armor, simply trudged on, one step after the other as hail stones bounced off their hard shells. By the time the storm ended, the tortoises had won the race.

Moral: Even bad weather can bring good results.

If you think the story ends there, well you haven't been paying attention, have you?

The next day the hares were worried and scared. Never had they seen such big hailstones, and there was nothing they could do about it. Before the next race they would have to prepare themselves, so the hares set to work building shells to protect them from falling hail. Not knowing much about shell design, they hired several tortoises to work with them. And not being very bright, they didn't realize that the tortoises they hired had their own personal interests in mind, so they recommended using only the heaviest materials.

For months the hares practiced running with their heavy shells, but even by the day of the race they couldn't manage to carry their shells as far or as fast as the tortoises, who had been toting them since birth. The race began and the tortoises pulled out into a brisk lead, while the hares struggled with their homemade shells. It was only when the hares were on the verge of exhaustion that one of them realized that it was a sunny day, and they didn't have to worry about hailstones. The hares abandoned their shells and raced towards the finish line. But it was too late; the tortoises had already won.

Moral: If you live in the past, you lose in the present.

Our story now moves 30 years into the future, when the original tortoise met the great–grandson of the original hare. You see, tortoises live to be over 50, but hares on average only live 8 years. Well anyway, by now they had all heard the stories of the tortoise–hare races. They were talking about the past, and the hare asked the old tortoise to tell him more stories about his great–grandfather.

"Well, I remember," said the tortoise as he rocked in his chair. "He was a friendly fellow, but unlike you, he was lazy and thought you could get through life taking shortcuts. When I won the race, it was a kind of wake up call for him. He gave up his lazy habits and went on to live a very good life. He refused to get involved in all the tortoise–hare races that followed, but set about to farm carrots for all the hares in the county. He was a rich hare too, because back then no hares had the patience to plant seeds and wait for them to grow. I once met him on the road and he thanked me for teaching him a lesson which changed his life."

They sat on the tortoise's porch and the hare thanked the tortoise and gave him a hug.

Moral: Time heals all wrongs.

If only stories would end when you want them to. Life would be so much simpler. We could relax and go to bed.

Fat chance.

You see, the original hare never learned from his experience. He went on to lose more races, and his laziness got him nowhere in life. He once even tried racing a flea and lost, because he didn't realize the flea had climbed onto his back and leapt off at the finish line. But the tortoise wanted the hare's great-grandson to be proud of his great-grandfather, so he made up the last story to inspire the young hare.

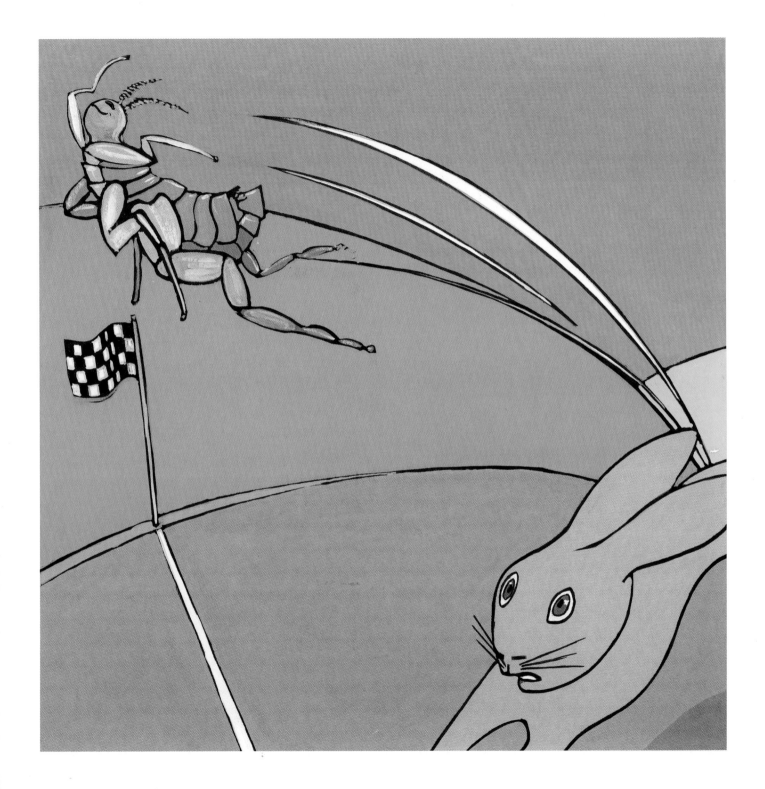

And years later, after the tortoise died, the hare's great-grandson grew up to be a famous doctor who worked hard with doctors of all species to build a better world for them all.

Once he spoke at a graduation and told the story of the tortoise and the hare, with the inspiring ending that the old tortoise had told him. The hares in the audience thought of all the good times they had when they should have been studying, and in their minds promised to live their days slower and steadier, like the hare in the story.

And you know, many did.

Moral: Made up stories can improve real lives.